My Forbidden Love

The Friends to Lovers Series

by

Reba Bale

Table of Contents

Anna 1

Jolene 5

Anna 8

Jolene 11

Anna 14

Jolene 17

Anna 21

Jolene 24

Anna 28

Jolene 32

Anna 35

Jolene 39

Anna 43

Jolene 46

Anna 50

Epilogue – Jolene 53

Special Preview 56

Other Books by Reba Bale 60

Copyright

---

1.   https://paperorpixels.com/

About This Book

There are just some things you don't do, like fall in love with your sister's ex!

Jolene never thought she'd fall for her sister's ex-girlfriend, but when the new neighbor turns out to be the same woman who broke her sister's heart, she can't help but feel drawn to her. As she spends time with her new neighbor, they become friends. But can they ever be more?

Anna always liked her ex's sister, but now that they're becoming friends, she's realizing she feels a little more than like. Sparks fly every time they're together. Jolene doesn't want to rock the boat with her sister, but when the passion erupts between them, they're going to have to figure out how to make things work.

Their love might be forbidden, but if feels so right...can they take their relationship to the next level without tearing Jolene's family apart?

"My Forbidden Love" is book ten in the "Friends to Lovers" romantic novella series. Each book in the series is a standalone story featuring an LGBT couple making the leap from friends to lovers and looking for their "happily ever after". If you like steamy but sweet romances with lots of snark, download this lesbian romance today.

Be sure to check out a free preview of Reba Bale's lesbian romance "The Divorcee's First Time" at the end of this book!

Dedication

This book is dedicated to everyone who's ever been in a relationship that was reality TV level awkward. Hoping it worked out.

Join My Newsletter

Want a free book? Join my newsletter and you'll receive a fun subscriber gift. I promise I will only email you when there are new releases or special sales, usually twice a month.

Visit my newsletter sign-up page at bit.ly/RebaBaleSapphic[2] to join today.

---

2. https://bit.ly/RebaBaleSapphic

Jolene

"Have you met your new neighbor yet?"

I sent Mrs. Lewis a smile. The older lady lived on the first floor of my building, right next to the mailboxes, and she kept an eye on everything that happened here. Some of the other tenants thought she was too nosy, but I recognized that she was just lonely. Instead of watching cable, she watched the lobby.

"No, not yet." I leaned one hip against her doorframe so she wouldn't have to shout at me from the recliner that had a direct line of sight through her open front door. "What do you know about her?"

"Not much. I just saw her briefly. A girl about your age, I think."

I suppressed a smile. At thirty-five, I wasn't often called a girl. Not anymore.

"Mr. Oliver said it's just one person on the lease. She's a referral from a former tenant."

Mr. Oliver was the owner of this building. I was pretty sure Mrs. Lewis had him on speed dial.

"Well, I'm sure I'll meet her eventually."

"In my day when you had a new neighbor, you'd bring over a pie or a casserole," Mrs. Lewis told me. "To welcome them to the neighborhood. I can't make it up the stairs or I'd go welcome her myself."

"That's not a bad idea. I was thinking about baking cookies tonight, maybe I'll make extra and go introduce myself to the new girl." I held up my hand as Mrs. Lewis opened her mouth. "Don't worry, I'll try to get the scoop on her and report back to you. I'll bring you down some cookies too."

I always shared my baked goods with her. I knew that she didn't have the money for luxuries. The only reason that Mrs. Lewis could afford to live in this neighborhood was because she'd been in her same apartment for thirty years.

The older woman sent me a grateful smile. "Thanks, dear."

A few hours later I crossed the hallway, a foil covered plate in my hand. I lived in a historic building on the south side of Seattle. It was a third-floor walk-up with four apartments on each floor. I'd lived here for about five years now and really loved it, even if the water pressure left a little bit to be desired.

I stopped in front of the door across the hallway, hoping I wasn't going to be disturbing my new neighbor. Personally, I didn't really like it when people just popped over to my house without an invitation. Then again, I couldn't just hang out in the hallway waiting for the new neighbor to wander by and accept my cookies.

Resolved, I knocked on the door.

"Coming!"

I heard a voice that sounded like it was coming from the back of the apartment, the bedroom probably. I was pretty sure that this apartment was a reverse copy of mine.

The lock clicked, and I automatically smiled, ready to greet my new neighbor.

The door opened, revealing a curvy body encased in paint-splattered jeans, ripped at the knees, and a tight tank top that didn't fully cover the dark pink sports bra underneath. I took in the long, thick brown hair, brown eyes, and the little space between the woman's front teeth as she returned my welcoming smile.

My smile dropped and I recoiled in horror as two things became immediately apparent: first, my neighbor was hot as shit. Second, my neighbor was no stranger. She was my sister's cheater ex-girlfriend.

Anna

When my friend Alice told me about this apartment that was opening in her old building, I'd jumped at the chance to move in. I'd spent the last year very awkwardly living with my ex-wife. That's right, we'd gotten divorced, but neither of us had moved out.

Don't get me wrong, the divorce had been mostly amicable, but until we could get the place fixed up and on the market, neither of us could afford anything in Seattle's pricey housing market. So we became roommates.

My ex, Melanie, had moved in with her new partner a few weeks ago, the day after we finally put the house on the market, and to both of our shock, the house had sold in only one day.

That left me no time to find a new house to buy. I'd put the word out to everyone in my network that I was looking for a short-term apartment to rent, and Alice had convinced the landlord of this place, Mr. Oliver, to offer me a six-month lease with an automatic renewal if I didn't find a place to purchase by then.

Now that I was living in an apartment again, I was re-thinking the idea of buying another house. The property taxes in this County were exorbitant, for one thing. And the idea of being able to call someone else when a light switch broke, or a pipe started to leak was very appealing.

I was painting my new bedroom when I heard a knock on the door. This was a security building, so I figured it had to be one of the neighbors coming over to say hello. Alice had mentioned that people in this building tended to be friendlier than most.

"Hi there," I said brightly as I opened up the door.

I hadn't seen the woman in the hallway in fifteen years, but I recognized her immediately. Jolene Schmidt. Her figure was fuller than it had been back then, her hair longer, and tiny lines bracketed her eyes, but I still knew it was her.

Jolene was my ex-girlfriend's little sister. Jess and I had dated in our early twenties, then had the most horrific break-up in the history of break-ups. At least that's what I thought at the time. I'd fancied myself in love with Jess, and the break-up had felt tragic. Fifteen years later, with the benefit of hindsight, I realized that although there had been a lot of passion between us, there'd been no depth. No love.

Jolene's mouth dropped in shock.

"Anna?"

"Jolene? Hi there. Long time no see. Do you live here in the building?"

She nodded, a litany of emotions passing across her face before her expression hardened.

"I live across the hall," she said dully. "I brought you cookies to welcome you to the building."

I reached for the cookies and she pulled them back, cradling the plate protectively against her stomach. Well, that was a bummer. I was starving.

"But that was before I knew who was living here."

I was surprised and maybe a little bit hurt by her vehemence. Jolene was three years younger than us, but we'd hung out with her frequently. The sisters were close, having both dealt with parents who were less than excited about both of their precious daughters being lesbians. I'd always really liked Jolene and had missed seeing her after her sister and I broke up.

"I've missed you. How have you been?"

A pink flush crept up her pale skin. "Don't talk to me like we're friends Anna, not after what you did."

"What did I do?" I asked. Surely, they still didn't believe...

"You cheated on my sister!"

"I did no such thing! Your sister broke up with me because *she* met someone else who tricked her into believing that I was cheating on her because she wanted Jess for herself. I was completely faithful to her."

"I was there Anna. I was there when she was on her couch sobbing about what you did."

"Was Angela there too? Comforting her?"

She frowned. "Yeah, so?"

"Angela lied to her. I tried to explain to Jess, but she wouldn't believe me. I was so hurt that your sister would believe someone she just met instead of the woman she'd been dating for over a year. That's when I realized then that what we had wasn't real, and I should just let her go."

Jolene looked unconvinced. Skeptical. Not that I blamed her. God knows her sister had been fooled by Angela too. That woman had the charm of a true sociopath. Suddenly Joleen sighed, as if she was exhausted.

"You know what? It doesn't matter. Here."

She pushed the cookies into my hand and turned to leave.

"Wait."

"What?"

"Did your sister date Angela after we broke up?"

"Yeah." She looked cautious, like she was trying to figure out where I was going with this.

"What happened? Are they still together?"

Jolene frowned.

"God no. Angela cheated on her too, with more than one person. And stole her credit cards. Then she tried to smear my sister's reputation with her friends by making up a bunch of shit about her."

"Oh, so you both realized that Angela was a liar, then?"

I could see the moment that my point landed. She looked at me, then looked up at the ceiling like she was looking for inspiration, then looked back at me.

"Oh."

"Yeah, oh."

She looked conflicted. She looked beautiful. And for the first time in what felt like a million years, I felt a jolt of attraction for someone else. It made me feel brave even though spending time with Jolene was probably a terrible idea. Not just because I'd dated her sister, but because she'd clearly spent the last fifteen years thinking that I was an asshole. Then again, I'd never been one to shy away from bad ideas.

"Can we get a beer sometime? Catch up, maybe?"

Jolene nodded slowly.

"How about tonight? In like an hour maybe?"

"That sounds good."

Jolene

While I waited for it to be time to meet Anna, I searched my memory for everything that happened when she and Jess had broken up.

I remembered thinking that they were an odd couple. Anna was always fun, artistic, a free spirit, while my sister was your typical "type A" personality, always planning, always trying to be in control. My sister used to joke around with us that I was much better suited for Anna than she was.

Then one night my sister messaged me that she and Anna had broken up. She'd heard from someone named Angela that Anna was sleeping with another woman. I'd rushed over to my sister's apartment to comfort her. We'd always been close, and I figured she'd need me. Angela beat me there.

With the benefit of hindsight, I could see now that Angela was a manipulative bitch. She seemed to play mind games with my sister and always had weird stories that never seemed to make a lot of sense. Like the story about Anna, who'd always followed my sister around like a puppy, kissing a woman on a street corner.

Worst of all, she tried really hard to isolate my sister from me. At the time I'd just thought she didn't like me, but later I realized that she didn't want anyone to find out her secrets.

It all came crashing down when Jess went to Angela's house and found her with someone else. It had been a man, and she'd tried to tell my sister that having sex with a man "didn't count" because she was really a lesbian. A few weeks after the break-up, Jess figured out that Angela had stolen her credit cards and ran them up to her limits. That's when another friend told her that Angela had been lying and cheating the entirety of their relationship.

She'd basically been running a con. Yet somehow, neither of us had ever reconsidered what had happened with Anna. Seeing Anna's face today, I couldn't help but believe her. I don't know why, but I knew in my heart that my new neighbor hadn't cheated on my sister.

Then again, maybe it was my hormones talking. I'd felt an instant rush of attraction the minute she'd opened the door, before I realized who she was. I'd always had a little crush on my older sister's girlfriend back in the day, but this felt different. Stronger. More grown up.

There was no way I was going to do anything with my sister's ex. But we could be friends, right? There was no harm in that.

We walked a few blocks to a bar called Miller's. It was one of those places that had been in the neighborhood for years, back when this part of Seattle had been a little grungy. Before there had been yoga studios and artisanal coffee shops on every corner. I greeted the owner, Big Bob, as we walked in. He made it a point to know all the regulars from the neighborhood.

"Hiya Jolene, how ya doing?" he called from across the bar.

"Hi Big Bob, I'm doing well. This is my new neighbor, Anna."

Big Bob gave her a friendly nod. "What can I get you girls?"

After ordering drinks, Anna and I settled in at one of the high tops along the back wall. It was a weeknight, and the bar was relatively quiet. If this was a Saturday, we'd never get a table.

I looked across the table at Anna. She'd changed out of her painting clothes, pulling on a loose cotton skirt, a scoop neck green tee shirt that brought out the olive in her skin, and a pair of those Teva sandals that everyone seemed to wear here in the summer.

I'd resisted the urge to change out of the faded jeans and tank top that I'd been wearing when I'd brought over the cookies. I didn't want Anna to think I was primping for her.

"What have you been up to the last fifteen years?" Anna asked carefully, as if she wasn't totally sure that I wasn't still mad at her.

"Well, after I finished college I got a job as an accountant at Phoenix Software. I've been working there ever since."

"Phoenix Software? You must know my friend Alice, she's an accounting manager there I think."

"Alice Abramson? Of course. She's actually my boss. That's funny that you know her too."

"Well as much as we all like to pretend otherwise, Seattle is still very much a small town in many ways."

"True."

Big Bob lumbered over with two beers and a basket of fries. "Here you go, give me a holler when you're ready for a refill."

"Will do, thanks."

Anna held up her drink. "A toast. To old friends, and new beginnings."

My eyes met hers across the table, a little arc of something passing between us. Electricity maybe. Awareness, definitely.

I broke eye contact to clink my glass against hers. "Cheers."

Anna

"How's single life treating you?"

"Technically I've been single for a year now."

My friend Alice waved her hand dismissively.

"You can't consider yourself single when you've been living with your ex-wife since the divorce."

"I can when my ex-wife was dating another woman most of that time."

Alice took a sip of her coffee. I'd invited her to meet me at the Morning Jolt coffee shop for lunch. It was near her office, and not far from mine, and they served the best coffee in the city, which was saying something in a city with a coffee shop on every corner. They also had great sandwiches and quiches you could get at lunch. Coincidentally, Alice's billionaire boss Madison owned the place.

"Do you like your new apartment?"

"Yeah, it's adorable and the owner gave me permission to spruce the place up with a coat of paint, so I'm having fun picking out colors and creating a space of my own. Thanks for helping me find that place."

When I'd gotten together with my ex-wife, I'd let her do all the decorating. Despite the fact that I was the artistic one, she had very definite feelings about how things were supposed to look. It was easier to let her have her way. I'd been seeing a therapist since the divorce though and I'd learned that I had a pattern of letting others set all the rules for my relationships. We were working on ways I could speak up for myself in relationships so I could avoid repeating the pattern again. Speaking of relationships...

"I understand you know my new neighbor," I told Alice. "Jolene."

"Jolene is your neighbor? That's great. She's awesome." Alice's eyes lit up. "Also, according to the office grapevine she's single. Do you think you two might..."

I held up my palm to stop her. "It's complicated."

"How is it complicated already? Didn't you just move in a few days ago?"

"We actually knew each other a long time ago. I used to date her older sister like fifteen years ago."

Alice rolled her eyes. "Jolene is your ex's little sister? So what? You may remember I married my best friend's little sister."

Alice had run into Jewel at a bar one night right after Jewel got out of the Peace Corps. Despite their seven year age difference, the two of them had fallen in love. It had been weird for the sister and the parents for a little while, but they'd gotten over it when they saw how perfect Alice and Jewel were for each other.

"Jolene's sister and I had a bad break-up. Jess became friends with this total sociopath who convinced her that I was cheating on her because she wanted her for herself. Then after Jess broke up with me, the chick cheated on her, robbed her blind, and tried to ruin her reputation."

"My God, this sounds like a soap opera, or one of those telenovelas."

"Seriously. I'd almost forgotten the whole thing, but then Jolene came over to my place to welcome me to the building and it all came up again. Apparently, this whole time Jolene and her sister have thought I'd screwed Jess over."

We paused as one of the baristas brought us the sandwiches we'd ordered to go with our coffee.

"You set things straight with Jolene, right?" Alice asked when we were alone again.

"Yeah I think so. I'm not sure if Jolene totally believes me, but she had to admit that if that woman lied and cheated and stole from her sister, it was very possible that she'd lied about me too."

"Obviously."

"Anyway, we're becoming friends. At least I think we are. We went for a beer the other night and have been texting a little. She's coming to my place tonight to watch a movie and eat pizza."

"Ooh, are you two going to 'Netflix and Chill'? Or watch a movie for real?"

"Watch a movie for real, Alice. I'm not going to put the moves on her."

"Why not? She's single, smart, in your general age range, and very attractive. Hell, I'd go for her myself if she wasn't my employee. Well, and if I wasn't with Jewel of course."

"We're just going to be friends."

When Alice continued to look at me skeptically I added, "Neither of us has seen the new Avengers movie yet. We thought we'd hang out and watch it together, that's all."

"What I hear you saying is that you're totally hot for her but you're too chickenshit to put the moves on her."

"How did you possibly get that out of what I said?" I asked incredulously.

Alice took a bite of her sandwich, chewing thoroughly before answering. "You know I'm like a lesbian relationship guru now, right? I've fixed up so many people, including my sister Rebecca. She and Heidi are getting married, you know."

We'd all heard the story about Alice's insistence that her sister go on ten first dates before going on a second date. Rebecca had come out after being married for years, and Alice had figured that would keep her sister from getting too serious too quickly. Apparently, her plan had worked, since Rebecca had met a woman named Heidi while on a date with another woman and they'd fallen in love.

"I really don't need a relationship guru Alice but thank you."

Alice snorted inelegantly. "Yeah sure, okay. I'll be here when you need me though."

Jolene

I was unaccountably nervous about hanging out with Anna tonight. I didn't know why. We were just going to order pizza and watch a movie. It wasn't like it was a date or anything. I hadn't seen Anna since we'd gone out for beers the other night, but we'd chatted by text several times.

The more I thought about it, the more I was embarrassed that neither Jess nor I had ever revisited the topic of Anna after the break-up with Angela. Jess was on vacation for two weeks but when she got back home, I was going to talk to her about it.

After fretting about my appearance more than I wanted to admit, I put on a pair of black leggings and a white Mariners tee shirt. The way you would if you were hanging out with a new friend on what was definitely not a date. I pulled my long blonde hair back in a low ponytail and grabbed the lemon bars I'd made earlier today.

I'd gotten into baking when I was just a kid. Both of our parents worked in high power jobs and were rarely home, leaving me and Jess to fend mostly for ourselves. Jess taught herself how to cook and I decided to learn how to bake, in deference to the serious sweet tooth we both had.

I was lucky to have a sister like Jess. She'd taken care of me as a kid and been my best friend as an adult. She'd also run interference when our parents decided that I was only saying I was a lesbian because it was 'a phase' and I was just 'copying' my sister.

Thinking back on the Anna and Angela situations though, I had to admit that for as good as my sister was in her relationship with me, her romantic relationships were less than stellar. There was always a lot of drama there. Even though she was thirty-eight now and old enough to know better, Jess was always falling in and out of love, often with big, dramatic break-ups. I was used to them now, but back when she and Anna broke up, it had been traumatic to see my sister sobbing and broken. But that had been a pattern that had repeated itself over and over again since then.

Maybe I should suggest my sister consider therapy. I knew a lot of people who'd successfully broken out of their bad relationship patterns with a little help. Anna had confided in me the other night that she was seeing a therapist for that very reason.

Anna opened the door before I even knocked.

"Oh hey, excellent timing. The pizza guy is here. I'm just going to grab it. Make yourself at home."

I walked into the apartment, looking around curiously. Anna had already unpacked everything in the main rooms, placing a large brown sectional around a low coffee table, a flat screen TV mounted on the wall across from the couch. Below the TV was a credenza with neatly arranged books. A glass and chrome table was perfectly centered in the dining area, a bowl of fruit in the middle.

I set the lemon bars on the counter that divided the kitchen from the dining room and sat at one of the stools. When Anna didn't immediately return, I pulled out my phone to check my email. I'd checked my Facebook notifications and moved onto Instagram before Anna finally returned, wielding a large pizza box. A container of salad was balanced on top.

"Everything okay?"

Anna smirked. "Mrs. Lewis waylaid me as soon as I got downstairs. The poor pizza guy practically ran off screaming from her interrogation, then she turned her attention to me."

"She's a sweet old lady," I defended. "Just lonely."

"Oh I know. I insisted that she take a couple of pieces of pizza and some salad. She's on social security and I'm sure that doesn't leave a lot of money for the little luxuries in life."

I was touched by how thoughtful Anna had been with our neighbor. She said it matter of factly, not like she was tooting her own horn or anything.

"What?"

Anna realized that I was staring at her.

"Nothing. It's just that...I forgot how kind you are."

She rolled her lips in like she was trying not to say anything. "Speaking of sweet, what did you bring us for dessert?"

"Lemon bars."

"Oh my God, I remember your lemon bars! Let's just forget the pizza and start with dessert!"

"Well, that is part of the fun of being an adult," I teased. "You can eat dessert first."

As I settled on the couch next to Anna, a plate full of Greek pizza in my lap, I had the strangest feeling that my life was about to change. I only hoped it was for good.

Anna

After our movie night, Jolene and I fell into a bit of a routine. Over the last two weeks we'd texted each other a few times a day, chatting about whatever was going on in our lives. One night I made way too much pasta and brought half of it over to Jolene, and twice she'd brought me baked goods.

Saturday morning we went to the Farmer's Market together, and Monday night I joined her at her regular yoga class. We were rapidly becoming good friends, and even though we'd only been back in each other's life for a couple of weeks, it felt like we'd been friends forever.

I was grateful for her friendship. My ex had gotten most of our mutual friends in the divorce, which made me realize that over the course of our marriage I'd gradually abandoned people who were just my friends only. It wasn't that my ex didn't want me to have friends, not exactly, but she got a bit pouty when I spent time with other people.

Now, with the benefit of both hindsight and my therapist, I could see that it was another way that I'd let myself and my needs get subsumed into my relationship.

"It's okay to have different interests and to express your own needs in a relationship," my therapist had told me. "It's actually healthy to individuate from your partner."

I've never fought for myself in a relationship. Jolene's sister Jess was a prime example. I knew I'd been lied about but when Jess told me she didn't want to talk about it, I just left. Accepted it. I'd wallowed in my hurt feelings rather than trying to defend myself. After growing up in a family where someone was always to blame, usually me, and being blamed led to emotional and physical abuse, I learned to just accept being treated like shit.

But not anymore. Now I was stronger. My self-esteem had never been stronger. And making a new friend, even if she was my ex's younger sister, felt like progress.

There was one little problem: I liked Jolene as more than a friend. I'd had a crush on her from the instant she showed up at my door with cookies the first day I moved in, but the more time I spent with her, the more I realized that what I felt was way more than friendship.

"Instead of monkey barring into your next relationship, try being friends with a woman you find attractive," my therapist advised. "It'll be a good experience for you to learn to separate attraction and other emotions like affection for a friend."

That wasn't the only reason I was determined to keep Jolene in the friend zone though. Having anything more than friendship with her felt just...wrong. She was my ex-girlfriend's sister. She'd hated me for years as a result of the break-up with her sister. My only other good friend was her boss. And she was my neighbor.

Jolene had 'forbidden' written all over her. If we entered into a romantic relationship and things went wrong, they'd go terribly wrong. Like telenovela or reality TV show wrong.

There was no way I wanted to put either of us through that. And now that I had Jolene as a friend, there was no way I wanted to lose her.

"Have you started dating yet?"

I looked up in surprise. Jolene and I were trying a new sushi place that had opened up near her office. She was still dressed in her professional accountant gear: a pencil skirt, blouse, and pumps. Her long blonde hair was pulled back in a sleek ponytail at the nape of her neck. It gave her kind of a sexy librarian vibe.

I'd also come from work, but since I worked in an auto parts warehouse, I was wearing jeans and a polo shirt. Together we looked like a vocational graphic comparing blue collar and white collar workers, I thought with a laugh.

"Since the divorce? No."

"Why not?"

"Well at first I was living with my ex, and that just felt all kinds of awkward. She only moved out recently and then the house sold super fast, as you know, and I had to move. There just hasn't been time."

Jolene looked thoughtful.

"Are you dating anyone?" I asked.

We hadn't talked about it, and I realized that I'd just assumed that she was single. She shook her head, and I didn't want to analyze too closely the feeling of relief that hit me.

"I got out of a relationship a couple of months ago. It was fine really, we just grew apart, but right now, I don't know, it just feels like too much trouble to date, you know? Like I'm so exhausted at the idea of dating I can't even contemplate trying again."

"Maybe we'll both stay single for the rest of our lives," I said, pointing my chopsticks at her. "We'll have to buy cats though."

"I'm allergic to cats."

"Oh sorry," I said with mock regret. "We can't let you in the 'no dating' club then."

Jolene

"How was your trip?"

My sister gave me a big smile. "It was great. I've got big news. I'm in love."

I resisted the urge to roll my eyes.

"Again?"

My sister fell in love with someone new at least four times a year. She was prone to big emotions and had a particular gift for falling in love with the exact wrong woman. If there was a lesbian who was a cheater, a thief, an abuser, or someone faking their identity anywhere in the Seattle metro area, there was a good chance that my sister had dated her.

I hadn't recognized this pattern with Jess back when things had gone down with Anna, but now I did. If the same thing happened today, I'd definitely be asking a lot of questions.

"This time it's real," my sister protested. "Be happy for me, Jojo."

I gave my sister a hug.

"I am happy for you Jess, it's just that...well, you've had a lot of bad relationships. You're so tender hearted. I worry about you."

I loved my sister, and she was one of my best friends. But her personal life was always a mess. She went from one bad relationship to the next, never single for more than a week or two, and every new relationship was the one she was convinced would be her forever love.

"This one is different. Katy is perfect for me."

She said this every time.

"Well in that case, I can't wait to meet her."

Jess made me dinner and then we sat at her battered dining room table and caught up on what had happened since the last time we'd seen each other. Jess had gone to Mexico for two weeks, where she'd met her new girlfriend at an all-inclusive resort. The woman lived in California though, so I wasn't sure how this would work.

"God, I've been jabbering on about myself all night. Tell me what's going on with you, Jojo."

"Well, I've got news."

Jess jumped out of her chair like she'd been electrocuted. "Oh my God! Are you in love?"

Unlike my sister, I tended to be super practical about relationships, avoiding anything dramatic or intense. And I'd never been in love.

I rolled my eyes. "No you idiot. Sit down."

"What's your news then?"

"Remember that woman you dated a long time ago, Anna?"

My sister's face hardened. "Oh yeah, I broke up with her because she cheated on me."

"Angela was the one who told you that Anna cheated on you, right? You never had any proof besides that, did you?"

My sister thought for a moment.

"No, I guess not. I remember Angela telling me that she'd seen Anna kissing another woman, and then she'd confronted the woman and she'd admitted that she and Anna were together. Then Angela told me."

"Given everything that happened with Angela after, the way she turned out to be a liar and a manipulator, did you ever wonder if she made the whole thing up?"

"No, not really. To be honest I haven't thought of Anna or Angela in years. Why do you ask?"

"Anna is my new neighbor," I said. "She moved into the apartment across the hall the day you went on vacation."

"No way! That's a weird coincidence. Have you spoken with her?"

"Yes. I was super angry with her at first, after what happened. But then she told me her side of the story and pointed out that the person who told you about her – lied about her she would say – was the same person who wanted you for herself. And then that person cheated on you and lied to you."

My sister looked confused.

"What are you saying? You don't believe that Anna ever cheated on me?"

"Not really, no. Angela clearly wasn't a credible source. Anna and I have hung out a few times over the last few weeks and, well, I just don't see it. Nothing about her says cheater."

My sister rested her chin on her hand as she considered my words.

"Well crap, now I don't know what to think. But if Anna didn't do anything wrong, why didn't she try to talk to me? Try to prove her innocence?"

"I suspect that she was too hurt at the accusations to defend herself but I don't know for sure."

"Maybe I should talk to her," Jess suggested. "Then we can bot get some closure."

"That might be a good idea."

"How has she been?"

"Pretty good, I think. She's divorced now after being married for almost ten years."

"Anna always wanted to be married," she said wistfully. "How does she look?"

"Beautiful." I didn't hesitate to answer. "She still has that thick dark hair. And a nice figure, a little curvier I think, but definitely a nice shape. She's aged well."

"Damn, she always was a hottie. And sweet as hell," my sister recalled. "If I didn't have a girlfriend, I'd be tempted to suggest that we give it another chance."

My gut churned with sudden jealousy, which was ridiculous. Anna and I were just friends, and that was all we would be. She was my sister's ex. My neighbor. Good friends with my boss. Anything other than friendship between us would be incredibly messy. Even if I was tempted. So tempted.

"You haven't seen her in fifteen years," I reminded my sister. "I'm sure you're two totally different people now."

"After I get caught up from my trip, maybe you can invite both of us over to get reacquainted. If nothing else, I probably owe that poor woman an apology."

Anna

Three months later...

"What do you think?"

I looked critically at the new couch that Jolene had just had delivered. The dark blue sectional was a little big for the space, but not terribly out of place. I dropped onto a cushion and gave it a few bounces.

"Much better. There's no butt divot and I don't have to avoid that spot that always felt like it was stabbing me in the ass."

Jolene and I had been nearly inseparable the last almost four months and I'd grown closer to here than I'd ever been to anyone, including my wife. There was an ease about our relationship. A lack of drama. A sense of mutuality that I found incredibly refreshing. My relationship with Jolene was different than any other relationship I'd had.

We had a routine. We texted every day, talking about whatever happened at work. We attended yoga classes and usually had dinner together once or twice during the week, either at Jolene's house or at a restaurant. On the weekends we went hiking, to the Farmer's Market, or just hung out and watched movies. Periodically we stopped by to visit with Mrs. Lewis on the first floor and hear all the gossip about other residents.

My therapist told me that this was what a healthy relationship looked like. The fact that I needed someone to tell me that was a clear illustration of the quality of my previous relationships.

Jolene sat on the next cushion, doing some bouncing of her own. I'd been teasing her about her ratty old couch ever since I started hanging out with her. The sad-looking piece of furniture had been so threadbare that she'd taken to covering it with a blanket. But the blanket hadn't hid the fact that all the cushions were compressed after years of sitting, and the frame creaked ominously every time you shifted on the thing.

"I don't know why I've been so hesitant to buy new furniture. I mean, I'm thirty-five years old and I have a good job, why have I kept this ratty old couch I've had since college?"

"Emotional attachment?" I suggested.

"No."

"Too lazy to go shopping?"

Jolene turned and smacked my shoulder. "Haha."

Her hand dropped to rest on my shoulder and our eyes met for a long moment. Immediately the air around us heated up, like someone had turned on the furnace. My shoulder felt electrified. This feeling of intense awareness happened a lot around Jolene, getting stronger the more time we spent together. When her guard was down, like right now, I could see she felt it too.

I knew instinctively that she was fighting it as much as I was, but I was tired of denying myself what I really wanted.

Maybe Jolene was too, because the hand on my shoulder slid down, her fingers wrapping around mine. My eyes locked on her face, and when she licked her lips, I couldn't help but groan softly.

"I really love our friendship," she whispered. "It means a lot to me."

"Me too."

"But sometimes..."

I knew what she was going to say before the words passed her lips.

"Me too."

Jolene nodded. "The thing is, I keep trying to fight these feelings I have when I'm around you but it's, well it's becoming harder and harder."

I knew in that moment that the easy friendship I'd shared with Jolene these last few months was about to change. I just wasn't sure if it would change for the better. I really hoped it would. But I felt like I should put up some resistance, just in case.

"I dated your sister. You've both hated me for years after."

Jolene had told me that Jess was now questioning what happened between us given Angela's actions after our break-up, but we'd yet to see each other. Even though Jess supposedly wanted closure, I never heard from her. I guess I could be the one to make the first move, but honestly, I was the wronged party here. It felt like Jess should be the one to initiate contact.

"Yeah, we did." Jolene's face was full of regret.

"I'm your neighbor. If things go wrong, we'll still have to see each other."

"Yeah."

"My best friend is your boss."

"Yeah." Joleen's other hand was now rubbing my knee.

"I'd hate to lose what we have."

"It's complicated. I get that as well as you Anna. But when I'm alone in bed touching myself, wishing it was you, wondering if you're touching yourself across the hallway at the same time while thinking of me, well, then it all feels less complicated."

Jolene scooted a little closer, but her eyes never left mine.

"The thing is, I've never felt this way before. I've never wanted to kiss anyone as much as I want to kiss you. The feelings have just gotten stronger over the last few months that we've been spending so much time together. And even though I've spent my entire life trying to avoid drama and complications, you're the complication I want."

Her words broke something in me. All the restraint that I'd held onto so closely over the last four months disappeared. I surged forward, my hands coming to her cheeks as I pressed my lips to hers in a hard kiss.

My entire body went up in flames. And in that moment, I knew instinctively that nothing in my life would ever be the same again.

Jolene

Anna kissed me with the unrestrained passion of someone who'd been denying themselves for too long. I knew the feeling. I felt like that cartoon guy who was in the desert and finally found water. The minute my lips touched Anna's I felt invigorated. Alive. And thirsty.

I pushed her backward and climbed on top of her, never breaking the kiss. I settled into place, my breasts pressing against hers, my fingers digging through her thick mass of hair as I deepened the kiss. My tongue swooped into her mouth, exploring. Conquering.

If Anna was surprised by my taking control, she didn't show it. She wasn't passive by any means, but she seemed content to let me lead. I pulled her hair a little just to reinforce my intentions, and she groaned against my mouth.

When I pulled away, we were both breathing heavily. I nipped along her jaw until my mouth was right by her ear.

"Have you ever been tied up?"

"N—no."

"Spanked?"

"No."

She shuddered but didn't recoil in horror like some other women I'd been with. Instead, she looked...interested.

I liked things a little rough. I got off by controlling my partners and giving them just enough pain to make things more intense. More pleasurable. I wasn't going to tie Anna to a cross and whip her, but I damn well wanted to see my mark on her while she begged me to let her come. Delaying orgasm was one of my favorite things to do.

I'm sure some therapist would say that my need to control everything in my life was a result of my chaotic childhood. I wasn't a purist, I didn't need to be in control one hundred percent of the time, but if the woman I was with couldn't let me lead most of the time, if she couldn't try a little light and playful BDSM, then things probably wouldn't work out for us.

I could do vanilla, but not all the time.

"I have this fantasy where I spank your ass until it's nice and pink then I tie you to my bed and ride your face until you make me come."

Anna made a choking noise at my filthy words. I took her earlobe between my teeth and bit down. Her pelvis rocked up against mine in response.

"Would you like that, baby?"

"God. Yes."

Levering off the couch, I grabbed her hand to pull her to standing. "Come with me."

I dragged Anna behind me until we got to the bedroom.

"Take off your clothes," I ordered, my voice firm.

She only hesitated a second before moving into action. I watched as she pulled her knit shirt over her head, then kicked off her shoes and shimmied out of her ancient jeans, leaving her standing in plain white cotton panties and a matching bra. The white fabric contrasted nicely with her olive skin.

"Keep going."

Anna reached behind her to unclasp her bra, sliding the straps down her shoulders before releasing her breasts from the cups. They were large and heavy, starting to succumb to gravity. Next, she removed her panties, revealing a pussy that was natural but trimmed. She squeezed her thighs together under my perusal and I knew if I touched her right now she'd be wet.

"I'm glad you don't wax," I told her huskily. "I hate women who look like little girls."

She nodded, a slight flush rising up her face.

"What about you?" she said, waving her hand in the general direction of my clothing.

"We'll get there."

I sat in the middle of the bed and patted my thighs. "Come here."

Her eyes widened, like maybe she thought I'd been kidding before when I asked if she was open to being spanked. I felt a rush of power when she crawled up the bed and sprawled over my lap, her bare ass centered over my thighs. I loved that she trusted me.

I rubbed the generous globes of her ass with my hands, stroking the silky skin, before I brought my palm down in a light slap. Testing her.

Thwack!

Anna gasped. I smacked her again, this time on the other cheek, then rubbed the skin to soothe it. She moaned softly. I knew it. I knew the minute I laid eyes on Anna that she had submissive tendencies.

Thwack!

This one was a little harder.

"You're the kind of person who spends a lot of time in their head, worrying about everyone else instead of your own needs. It's why you've let people walk all over you your whole life."

Thwack!

Thwack!

"Right now, we're going to focus on your needs Anna. I want you to give yourself over to the sensations. Submit to me like a good girl and I'll make you feel good."

Thwack!

Thwack!

A slight pink flush was rising on her ass, giving me a sense of satisfaction. I could almost make out the outline of my fingers.

Thwack!

Thwack!

I gradually increased the pressure, making my smacks more forceful as her skin warmed up. I watched in fascination as the flesh of her ass compressed with every touch of my hand.

Thwack!

Thwack!

Her breathing was changing, little moaning noises coming from her throat that she likely wasn't aware of as she gave herself over to the pleasure that arose from the quick bite of pain.

Thwack!

Thwack!

When Anna was lifting her ass to meet my hand I stopped, sliding my fingers between her ass cheeks and down to her pussy. She was dripping wet. She widened her legs slightly, seeking pressure, and I chuckled darkly.

"On your back."

Anna

No one had ever spanked me before. I'd never even considered that to be a thing I would like. Spanking scenes were always hot in romance books, but I figured they were fantasy. Pain could never feel that good.

Apparently I was wrong. Because every time Jolene's hand came down on my ass it sent a jolt of excitement straight to my clit. The skin on my ass felt heated and I was almost embarrassed by how wet I was right now. I could feel the moisture dripping down between my thighs and onto the bed. No doubt Jolene could too.

"On your back."

I couldn't help but obey. Jolene had been right before. I'd always focused on everyone else, both in and out of the bedroom. Giving over control of my pleasure to someone else would be a new experience, but I was dying to try it.

While I shifted onto the bed, Jolene rummaged in her closet, returning with a few belts hanging over her arm. I gasped, causing her to smile indulgently.

"I'm not going to whip you with a belt, silly girl."

She reached over my head and pulled up my hand, securing my wrist to the headboard with one of the belts, then did the same with my other hand. I pulled on my bonds, noting that they were secure. I could move my arms, but not a lot.

"You can't come until I give you permission."

"What?" I choked, close to coming just from her words.

"Be a good girl and wait for my permission and I promise that I'll reward you. Now open wide."

She tapped the outside of my thigh. I spread my legs and she pulled them open even more, affixing them one by one to the bedframe. Jolene was still fully dressed and here I was, totally naked, spreadeagled and tied to the bed. My face burned with humiliation at being in this vulnerable position, and yet I could feel my nipples hardening and my heart racing with excitement.

Jolene climbed on top of me and kissed me hard. When she bit my lower lip, I opened for her eagerly and she kissed me until my lips were swollen and my pussy was clenching on air, desperate for something more to happen.

Sliding her way downward, Jolene sucked one of my nipples into her mouth. She circled it with her tongue while she scraped her fingernail around the other one. When she bit down on my nipple I cried out in pain, then damn near came from pleasure. After giving my other breast the same attention, she gave me a smile that made me feel a mixture of apprehension and excitement.

"Next time I'm going to clamp these nipples and get them good and hard."

I shivered.

She kissed her way down my belly, then settled between my legs, licking up the inside of one thigh, then the other, avoiding where I needed her to be. This experience was so hot, so erotic, that I couldn't form a coherent thought. My mind was focused on one thing and one thing only: my desperate desire to come.

"Please," I gasped.

Jolene looked up from between my legs.

"What do you need, baby?" The glimmer of amusement in her eyes told me she knew exactly what I needed.

"I want to come. Please. I need to come."

I hadn't had an orgasm with another person in longer than I could remember. My ex-wife and I had lost interest in the sexual part of our relationship years ago and while I'd taken care of myself with a vibrator, nothing compared to this.

She slid one exploratory finger through my channel.

"I don't think you're ready yet," Jolene said.

And then, God help me, she bit one of my pussy lips. I yelped, my hips punching up. She slid her tongue into my channel, lapping up my moisture, then placed a bite on the other side. The altering sensations of pain and pleasure were driving me wild. I thrashed against my restraints and Jolene lifted her head, giving my pussy a hard smack.

"Be a good girl."

I stilled instantly, and she nipped along the sensitive skin of my inner thigh, leaving stinging bites that just made me hotter. When she finally returned her attention to my pussy, I sighed in relief.

She slid one long finger between my lower lips, stroking up and down my channel, her finger becoming firmer with each pass. Then she circled that finger around my opening and pushed it inside me. My inner muscles clenched around her, desperate to be filled. She added a second finger and then a third, stretching me wide enough to sting, then started roughly fucking me with her fingers while I bucked against her hand.

I was close. So close. But I needed more.

"Please. Now. Please." I was begging now, certain I was going to die if I didn't get relief.

"Ask me nicely."

"Please Jolene, please let me come." My voice sounded as desperate as I felt.

Finally – finally – she lowered her head and took my throbbing clit into her mouth, teasing it with her tongue. Her fingers curved, finding my G-spot, as her tongue pressed harder against my clit.

And then I was flying. My orgasm barreled down my body, lighting every nerve ending it passed on the way. My back bowed, my hips bucked, and my arms and legs pulled at the restraints as I screamed in pleasure.

Jolene kept stroking me through my first orgasm until a second one, even deeper and harder than the first, overtook me. I was sobbing now, tears dripping down the side of my face, a jumble of nonsensical words falling from my mouth with every breath.

When she finally lifted her head and removed her fingers from my body I sagged into the mattress, gasping for breath and wondering how the hell I was ever going to recover from this.

Jolene

Anna letting go was a beautiful sight to see. It made me hotter than I'd ever been. After I wrung two orgasms out of her just to make doubly sure that she was good and sated, I hopped off the bed and practically ripped my clothes off.

My clit was so swollen right now that moving was painful, and when I removed my panties the crotch was soaked right through. I'd been with a fair number of women since I'd come out as a lesbian, but no one had ever made me feel this desperately needy before.

She opened her eyes as I climbed on the bed, crawling up her body. Her gaze was unfocused, and I couldn't help but give her a long kiss before I sat up, straddling her belly.

"Oh my God. Thank you. I've never come that hard in my life," she confessed.

Her face was softer right now, free of that worried look she wore like a mask. I could tell she was too wrung out from her orgasms to worry about anything other than what came next.

"You're going to make me come now," I said, reaching up to free her hands.

"Gladly."

She shook out her arms, making me wonder if maybe I'd bound her too tight, and I ran my lips around one wrist and then the other, soothing the sting of the leather that had pressed against her sensitive skin. Her wrists were a little red, but it was already fading.

"You have to tell me if I tie you up too tight," I said firmly. "You should only feel good pain."

"It wasn't too tight. I liked it."

Her voice was rough from screaming her way through two orgasms. I hoped the downstairs neighbors hadn't heard. But then again, thinking of them listening to me make Anna come was kind of hot.

I wondered if she'd be down for a little exhibitionism. I could see me taking her in the woods while people hiked nearby, or maybe controlling her with a bullet vibrator buzzing in her pussy while we ate dinner in a restaurant. The possibilities were endless.

Shifting to straddle her head, I gripped the edge of the headboard and slowly lowered myself down until I was hovering just above her face. Anna grabbed my hips and pulled me the rest of the way down, until I was sitting on her face. Her tongue flicked out, licking me from bottom to top, and I shivered.

Had I ever been this aroused? This desperately horny? I didn't think so.

Humming against my folds, she moved back and forth through my channel licking up my cream like it was her last meal on Earth.

I cried out as her rough tongue moved to circle my engorged clit, circling it until I was close to begging her to make me come the way I'd made her beg me. The bundle of nerves was so sensitive right now that it was almost painful, and I could feel my pulse fluttering and making it throb.

Just when I couldn't take it anymore, Anna licked downwards until her tongue found the opening of my channel, thrusting inside me.

I ground against Anna's face as she fucked me with her tongue. I was already so close. It felt like the last four weeks had been foreplay, everything leading up to this moment. Then seeing my handprints on her ass, tying her down and watching her surrender to me so completely, it was the single hottest thing I'd ever experienced.

Closing my eyes, I visualized Anna's face as she came for the second time, tears streaming down her cheeks from the intense emotions.

Then, without any warning, she reached around me and pinched both of my nipples between her fingers at the exact same time. Meanwhile she kept vigorously thrusting into me with her tongue, working it in as deep as it would go. When her tongue curled inside me, I lost all control.

"Anna!"

I bucked against her face, knowing I had to be cutting off her air at least a little bit, and not caring because all I could focus on was the waves and waves of pleasure coursing through my body.

Beneath me, Anna continued licking up my moisture as I came in a rush. I realized to my shock that I was actually squirting. I'd thought that was a myth, but damned if this woman hadn't brought it out of me. By the time my orgasm receded I was wrung out, sore, and happier than I'd been in a long time.

I pried my fingers off the headboard and, swinging my leg over Anna, crawled to the bottom of the bed to release her ankles, rubbing the slight redness there from her pulling against the restraints.

When I glanced back up, she was watching me with a tiny smile. I shifted to lay my head on her shoulder, one arm over her belly, one leg wrapped over hers. We lay there quietly for a long time until Anna finally spoke.

"I didn't know it could be like that."

I looked up so she could see the truth in my eyes. "Neither did I. That was, hands down, the hottest sexual experience of my entire life."

She gave me a smile that lit up her face, and I realized that now that she was coming out of her post-orgasm haze, she was likely feeling a little insecure. I vowed then and there to make sure that she never felt 'less than' in a relationship again.

Because no matter how complicated it was going to be, I planned to spend the rest of my life with this woman.

As we snuggled together in that place between wakefulness and sleep, I wondered how we were going to make it all work.

Anna

"What's new?"

I eyed my friend Alice across the table.

"I need to talk to you about something."

"Okay." She put her coffee down and gave me her full attention.

"I know it might be awkward, but you are literally the only person I can talk to about this so please, reserve judgement."

"You're freaking me out, Anna. Did you commit a crime? Give someone a venereal disease? Hit on my wife?"

"Please, like Jewel has eyes for anyone besides you."

Alice and Jewel were blissfully happy and despite their apparent differences, they fit together perfectly.

"I know that," Alice said smugly. "But that doesn't mean people don't try to hit on her. She's a very beautiful woman."

"I did not try to hit on your wife," I said firmly. "But I did have sex with one of your employees."

Her eyes widened.

"You and Jolene had sex?" she whisper-shouted.

"I knew it! I knew you had a crush on her, but you were all like," she pitched her voice higher in what was supposed to be an imitation of me, "oh no, we're just friends, we don't see each other like that."

I leaned back in my chair. "Turns out we do."

"Well, don't hold out on me. How was it?"

"Life changingly good. And scary."

"Scary? Why? What's the problem?"

"There's no problem, really, other than I'm pretty sure I'm falling in love with her, and I suspect her sister is going to freak out when she finds out that we're together."

Alice waved her hand dismissively. "You two dated a million years ago."

"Still, would you want to hear that you and your sister had sex with the same woman? It's creepy."

Alice shuddered.

"I admit, it is a tad bit creepy, but it was also what? Fifteen years ago? You were barely adults back then. When did you and Jolene finally do the deed?"

"Two days ago."

We paused as the barista brought us sandwiches to go with our coffee.

"No wonder she's been so cheerful at work the last couple of days. What happened after?"

"We fell asleep in each other's arms, woke up in the middle of the night to have sex again, fell asleep again, went to work, came home and had sex again – twice – and here we are."

"Wow." Alice fanned her face. "That sounds hot."

I debated my next words, desperate to talk to someone about my fears. I could talk to my therapist about this, but I was afraid of how she might react. Alice was one of the most open and non-judgmental people I knew. If I could talk to anyone about this, it was her.

"There's one thing." I leaned closer and lowered my voice. "And this is where I need you to forget she's your employee for a minute because I don't know who else to talk to about this."

Alice mimicked my position, leaning closer. "What is it?"

"Um. Let me ask you a question. Do you and Jewel ever...do anything rough?"

"Rough?"

I could feel my face flaming. "You know. Like spanking. Or tying each other up."

Alice leaned back with a laugh. "Oh God yeah, all the time. My little wife is quite the domme."

"Are you saying that Jewel...?"

I was shocked. Jewel was seven years younger than Alice, and sweet as could be. If anyone was dominant in that relationship, I would have expected it to be Alice.

"We're not into hardcore BDSM if that's what you're asking. She doesn't whip me or walk me around on a leash or anything. But yeah, Jewel likes to be in control, and I like it when she is too. When she's in charge, when she adds a little pain to the pleasure, it's the one time I can completely shut off my mind and just...feel. It's a total high."

"Really?"

Alice's casual attitude about this was making me feel better about letting Jolene tie me up. And spank me. And fuck my ass with a butt plug while I was on my hands and knees wearing a blindfold and nipple clamps.

My friend studied me carefully, as if she could read my thoughts.

"Oh I see, Jolene is a little kinky and you've been strictly vanilla up til now, is that it?"

"Yeah."

"Are you worried that it's weird that you like submitting? Is that what you're worried about?"

I nodded, relieved that she understood.

"I don't know, maybe it's the feminist in me, maybe it's just how I was raised, but on some level, it feels wrong how much I like the things she does. How much I like to be dominated."

"Look, if you both like it and you're getting off on it, there's absolutely nothing wrong with two consenting adults doing what feels good. As long as she's not controlling you in other ways...?"

I shook my head.

"Or hurting you – actually hurting you I mean, like injuring you or beating you or something?"

"No, nothing like that."

"Well in that case, you've found a unicorn. You'd better hold onto that girl."

The tension left my body in a whoosh.

"Thanks Alice, I feel much better now."

"I'm glad you do. But now there's no way I'm going to be able to look at Jolene in our staff meeting this afternoon."

Jolene

It had been a month since Anna and I had moved our relationship to a sexual one, and I'd never been happier. We were perfectly compatible both inside and outside of the bedroom. She slept over here almost every night, and we were still in that 'can't get enough' phase of an early relationship.

Anna stirred in my arms and I curved myself around her back, surrounding her.

"Good morning," I whispered, pressing a kiss against her shoulder.

"Good morning," she mumbled, her voice rough with sleep.

It was a Sunday morning, and we had nowhere to be, which was good because I'd woken up incredibly horny.

I pressed one knee between hers and she opened her legs, letting me wedge her legs open wider with my thigh. I slid my hand slowly from her hip, sliding up her nightshirt, gratified to find that she hadn't put any panties on after we'd had sex last night.

I cupped her mound, then gave it a little squeeze that made her sigh. I loved the way she surrendered to me almost instantly.

"You know what I want?" I said softly, squeezing her mound tighter.

"What?"

"I want you to come on my hand."

Slipping my fingers between her lower lips, I could feel her growing wet already. I moved back and forth a few times, getting her ready, then grabbed her top leg, pulling it back more so I could open her up wider for me.

Gently, I tapped my fingers against the top of her pussy, right over her clit. I continued tapping until she ground her ass back against me then I smacked her a little harder, this time using my entire hand.

Her moan was gratifying. I smacked her pussy sharply a couple more times, then without saying a word I shoved one finger as deep as I could into her channel. She clenched around me, always greedy, and I added two more fingers to fill her up the way she liked.

She was using my arm as a pillow, so I bent my elbow until I could wrap my hand around her throat. I pressed just enough to remind her that I was in control while I continued to roughly fuck her with my fingers.

"Jolene. God."

"You know the rules, baby. You can't come until I give you permission."

Unfortunately for her, I'd woken up in a teasing mood. She was going to have to work for her orgasm. We'd both enjoy that.

I waited until I felt her inner muscles starting to spasm against my fingers, signaling that her orgasm was close, then I pulled out. She groaned in frustration, and I briefly tightened my other hand that was on her throat, to remind her who was in charge.

"Hands and knees," I ordered.

She scrambled over, her heavy breasts tenting out her nightshirt where they hung unencumbered.

Moving to sit on my heels, I slid her nightshirt up to her waist, then smacked her bare ass sharply.

Thwack!

I moved to the other cheek, giving it the same treatment.

Thwack!

Anna moaned. My girl loved her spankings.

Thwack!

Thwack!

I gave her a few more sharp spanks, waiting until her skin was nice and pink before changing position.

"Widen your knees a bit."

She did as instructed, and I reached one hand underneath her to stroke her clit. My other hand slid inside her channel, gathering moisture before I moved to trace the puckered hole of her ass. She gasped as I slid one finger in, just to the first joint, and started pumping it in and out.

Shifting my attention from her clit, I went back to her vaginal opening, until I had one finger stroking in and out of her pussy in tandem with the finger stroking in and out of her ass.

"Please. Jolene, I need to come so bad."

"Not yet greedy girl."

I removed both hands and spanked her a little more.

Thwack!

Thwack!

Her elbows gave out, her chest dropping to the bed, cheek smashed into the mattress even while she kept her ass in the air.

I reached over to the nightstand and Anna groaned loudly, knowing what was coming. Hitting the button one of the many vibrators I kept in there, I brought it to her clit. Pressing one hand to the small of her back to keep her still, I used the vibe on her clit until she was begging me to come, then thrust it inside her channel. It was huge, but she was so wet now that it slid in easily.

"Please may I come? Please may I come?" she chanted.

"I love it when you beg me," I teased.

She'd had enough edging for one morning.

"Yes, you can come," I said.

Leaning over, I sunk my teeth into the skin of her ass cheek while thrusting the vibrator inside her as deep as it would go.

For an instant Anna went completely still, then she let out a scream that would wake the dead. She pressed backwards, fucking herself against the vibe and shuddering so hard I was afraid she'd fly right off the bed. I grabbed her hip with one hand, grounding her as she rode out her orgasm.

"Jolene! Fuck! Ohhh Jolene!"

I turned off the toy, sliding it out of her gently and tossing it towards the edge of the bed while Anna collapsed on her stomach, still shuddering from the intensity of her orgasm.

"Oh my fucking God," she mumbled against the mattress. "I'm going to need a few minutes to recover."

Anna

I was still buzzing from that incredible orgasm when Jolene rolled over onto her back next to me.

"My turn."

With difficulty, I pushed myself up to my elbow. She'd removed her pajamas while I was recovering and was now delightfully naked. My eyes roved over the soft curves of her body, lingering on her full breasts and the thatch of blonde hair at her apex.

"Get the Magic Wand. I want to come hard and fast."

The Magic Wand was the heavy-duty vibrator, the one that was guaranteed to send you into the stratosphere in less than sixty seconds if you used it right. I rolled over to grab it out of the drawer, hanging off the side of the bed to plug it in.

Thwack!

"Ow!"

The smack on my ass was unexpected. And it made my body tingle despite the fact that I'd just come so hard I'd nearly blacked out.

"You're moving too slow," she teased.

I took the head of the monster vibe and slid it between her lips, halfway between her clit and her opening, just the way she liked it. Turning it on low, I pressed it against her pelvic bone, then shifted so I could give her a kiss.

Our tongues tangled for a few minutes while I held the vibe steady, getting her ready. Moving downward, I caught one hard nipple in my mouth, sucking on her little bud and making it even harder than it was.

Slowly I shifted the vibrator closer to her clit. You needed to work up to that a bit with a vibrator this powerful, and I moved it up and down slowly. Every time I brushed the edge of the wide head against her clit, Jolene punched up her hips and moaned.

Kissing my way down her body, I nibbled on her hip as I continued to tease her clit. Getting me off the way she had would have made Jolene incredibly aroused already – she usually came really quickly after a scene like we'd just had—but I was trying to prolong her pleasure a little bit longer.

"Quit fucking around," she ordered, her tone impatient.

I chuckled. I guess that was enough prolonging.

I put the head of the magic wand directly onto her clit, pressing down. Jolene bent her knees, opening herself wider and bucking against the vibe.

"Fuck. Fuck. Fuck."

I gripped her hip so I could keep the toy steady and within seconds Jolene succumbed to her orgasm. I glanced down, seeing her toes curl under and her fingers grip the sheets beneath her until they were white. Her hips shifted up and down as I followed her with the Magic Wand until she shrieked, a flood of moisture practically bursting out of her pussy.

Turning off the toy, I slid between her legs and licked it up. Her fingers curled into my hair as she rode out the aftershocks.

"Good girl."

It turned out that I had a praise kink because every time Jolene called me a 'good girl' I wanted to throw myself at her feet and pledge my obedience to her forever.

"Get up here."

I moved up the bed, laying next to her, and she rolled us over until she was laying on me like a blanket, her hips between my legs, our bare pussies pressed together, her head resting in the crook of my shoulder.

Joleen and I rested like that for a long time until we heard a loud gasp. We both jumped, and Jolene rolled off me. We sat up to meet the shocked eyes of Jolene's sister. She clamped her hand over her eyes.

"Oh my God!" she screeched dramatically. "I did not need to see my sister's shiny white ass this morning!"

"Dramatic much?" Jolene asked with deceptive calm.

Jess peeled her hand down, taking in the scene once again, this time her eyes going to my face and widening almost comically.

"Anna? What the fuck? You're sleeping with my ex-girlfriend, Jolene? I can't believe this shit!"

We heard the door slam as she stormed out of the apartment.

Jolene

I dropped to my back with a long sigh. Damn it, this was not how I wanted my sister to find out about me and Anna. It was my own fault of course. Our relationship had changed over a month ago, but I'd avoided broaching the topic with my sister even though I talked to her almost every day.

When I'd first brought up that Anna was my neighbor, it had sounded like Jess was open to getting together with Anna and hearing her side of the story. Accepting that if Angela lied about so many other things, she'd likely lied about Ana as well.

But then it turned that the woman my sister had met in Mexico wasn't all that she said she was, and Jess had been in one of her "all women suck" moods for a few weeks until she found another person to hook up with. By that time, I'd decided just to let sleeping dogs lie.

Then when Anna and I had started sleeping together, I'd been too nervous to bring it up; I'd never even told her that we were hanging out as friends.

"I take it your sister didn't know about us?" Anna said quietly.

"Not exactly."

She turned her head and gave me a stern look. I might have dominated her in the bedroom, but she could hold her own outside. I'd seen her grow more and more confident just in the few months since she'd moved in across the hall. She was less passive, more vocal about her own needs. I knew that her work with her therapist had helped her immensely, but I liked to think our relationship had been beneficial as well.

"Are you going to go talk to her?"

I put my arm over my eyes. "I don't wanna," I whined.

She pulled my arm back. "Do you want me to go with you?"

I lifted my head to give her a quick kiss. "No, I probably should handle this alone. But thank you."

Anna got out of bed, looking around until she found where she'd left her panties last night.

"Okay, I'm heading home but let me know how it goes."

"I will."

I took a long shower, both to clear my head and to clean up from two vigorous rounds of lovemaking since we'd gone to bed last night. I didn't bother texting my sister that I was coming, I knew she knew that I'd come over and she knew that I knew she'd be waiting for me. I was right.

I used my key to get in, the same way she'd done for my place, and found her sitting at the dining room table sipping a cup of coffee. She looked much calmer.

"Are you decent?" I asked wryly as I entered, heading towards the kitchen to get a cup of coffee for myself.

"Are you?" she shot back.

"Well now, it's a little late for that question."

"Yeah I know, I'm sitting here considering bleaching my eyes."

I sat across from her with my coffee. "Next time let me know you're coming."

"I texted you and when you didn't answer, I assumed you were sleeping in. I thought we could go to brunch. But then I saw you'd already eaten."

I snorted at her joke.

"Why didn't you tell me you were seeing someone? Or was it just a one-time thing?"

"Are you more upset about who I'm sleeping with or that you didn't know there was someone in my life?" I asked.

"Honestly? It was a shock to see Anna. I remember you saying she'd moved in across the hall from you but then you never mentioned her again and I forgot all about her. Until I saw you humping her this morning."

"I wasn't humping her. We were...snuggling."

My sister rolled her eyes.

"How long has this been going on?"

"We've been friends since she moved in four or five months ago. We became, um, intimate, about a month ago."

"Is it serious?"

I nodded. "I love her. She's the one, Jess. I want to spend the rest of my life with her."

"Wow, I guess it is serious. Your whole life I've never heard you say you were in love." My sister's eyes filled with tears. "I'm just sad, Jojo. I always thought we told each other everything."

I moved around the table to give her a hug, then dropped into the chair closest to her.

"I'm so sorry Jess, I didn't mean to hurt you. Truly I didn't," I explained. "It's just, well my relationship with Anna is ridiculously complicated. It's like something out of a bad TV show. Not only is she my neighbor and my sister's ex-girlfriend, but her best friend is my boss."

Jess frowned. "Is your relationship with Anna actually complicated though? Everything you're mentioning is about external factors."

I shook my head. My sister was dead-on in her assessment.

"My relationship with her is the simple part," I said softly.

"How does Anna feel? Is she in love with you too?"

I didn't meet my sister's eyes.

"Maybe? We haven't really talked about it. You know I'm not one to leap into things."

"It looks to me like you already leapt. If you're really in love with Anna, you should be telling her that before you tell me or anyone else."

"Are you upset about who it is though?" I asked. "You didn't answer."

She shook her head. "Not really. I was just surprised back there. I thought about it on the way home, and I truly believe that Angela fucked us over back then. Anna should have fought for me, but I shouldn't have let myself be manipulated like that."

She paused to take a long drink of her coffee.

"But then again, maybe it's good we broke up when we did. Remember how I always joked that you two had so much more in common than Anna and I did? It would have been even more awkward if I'd still been dating her when the two of you fell in love, that's for sure."

"Yeah, that would have taken this whole shit show to a brand new level," I laughed.

"I'm sorry that I barged in on you guys like that. Believe me when I say I'll knock next time. Loudly."

"You're just lucky you didn't come fifteen minutes earlier or you really would have seen a show."

"Gross! You're my baby sister, stop!"

Anna

I'd been pacing across my apartment for two hours now. I had stuff to do, but right now I couldn't seem to do anything but walk back and forth, my head creating any number of terrible scenarios.

Was Jolene going to break up with me now? I had no doubt that if she had to choose between me and her sister, she'd choose her sister. Those two had always been super close. Jolene and I had talked a lot about how her sister had taken care of Jolene when they were growing up, and how Jess had been the only one in the family who supported her when she came out as a lesbian. Although that was probably because Jess had done it first and already broken ties with everyone besides her sister anyway.

It had been hard to see the look of disgust on her sister's face when she'd walked in on me and Jess. I'd done a lot of work since the divorce, building up my self-esteem and figuring out how to have healthier relationships.

My relationship with Jolene was the best relationship I'd had in my entire life. It was built on respect and mutual support and yes, great sex. I'd been worried when we first started sleeping together that things would change with our friendship. That maybe Jolene would be as controlling outside the bedroom as she liked to be inside, but those fears had been unfounded.

She was the same Jolene that I'd become such close friends with. In fact, she actively encouraged me to speak up, to share my thoughts, and to express my opinions even if they were different from hers.

I'd also learned that being dominant is what helped her get off during sex, and conveniently, being dominated helped me get off too. It was everything I never knew I needed.

If I lost it, if I lost the woman I loved, I didn't know what I was going to do.

I nearly jumped out of my skin when I heard a knock on the door. I hurried over, not even looking through the peephole. I already knew it would be Jolene.

"Hey," she said, her face unreadable. "Can I come in?"

"Of course."

I went to the fridge and got two bottles, handing one to her before joining her on the couch. She took a long drink and when I couldn't stand it anymore, I blurted out, "Are you going to break up with me?"

Jolene choked on her water. She put the cap back on the bottle before meeting my eyes.

"I'm not here to break up with you, Anna. I'm here to tell you that I love you."

I reared back in shock. "I don't understand."

"What don't you understand? I love you. I'm *in* love with you. And maybe it's too soon, but I just want to put it out there that I want to spend the rest of my life with you."

"But your sister..."

"Is fine with it. Not that it's up to her, but she is. And she wants to get together with both of us one night this week so we can clear the air about the past."

"I saw her face, Jolene. I heard what she said. She was really upset to find me in bed with you."

"Apparently, she was more upset about the fact that she didn't know I was dating someone than she was about that someone being her long-ago ex-girlfriend. Also, she was traumatized by seeing my naked ass."

"You have a great ass," I defended.

She smirked. "My sister doesn't think so I guess."

When I didn't say anything else, her expression turned uncharacteristically vulnerable.

"Did you hear what I said earlier? The part where I said I love you and want to spend the rest of my life with you? I mean, no pressure if that's not where you are right now, but it would be great if you can at least tell me that we're heading in that direction."

"I told my therapist that I was in love with you a couple of weeks ago, and she thought maybe I was jumping in too fast," I admitted. "It made me nervous to say anything to you."

"Does it feel too fast to you?"

"No, does it feel too fast to you?"

"Nope."

"In that case," I reached out to take both of her hands. "I love you too Jolene. And I want nothing more than to spend the rest of my life with you."

We moved forward at the same time, our lips meeting in the middle, kissing until we were both breathless. I pushed her gently backwards, then settled myself on top of her, as if reassuring myself that she wasn't going to leave.

"You think you get to be in charge now?" she teased, lifting her head to nip at my chin.

"That's right."

"Well, maybe just this once," she said with mock reluctance.

"That's okay, as long as you love me, I'll always let you be the boss in the bedroom."

"Really?"

"Really."

Jolene's smile was pure evil. "That's great, because I've been wanting to try out this new toy..."

Epilogue – Jolene

Six months later...

"Are you sure we're ready for this? It's a big commitment."

I took Anna's hand in mine and took a deep breath.

"We can do it. I'm ready."

"Okay then, let's go."

We opened the door and were immediately assaulted with a cacophony of sounds. I wrinkled my nose at a smell that was a combination of disinfectant and urine. An elderly woman sat behind the desk, her face creasing into a welcoming smile.

"Welcome to the Seattle Humane Society, how can I help you today?"

"We want to adopt a dog," Anna said. "A puppy."

"That's great, I'll just need you to fill out some paperwork, then I'll take you back and introduce you to some of our guests."

Two hours later we emerged from the building with a large bag of dog food, two bags full of supplies, and a pair of geriatric bulldogs.

"I can't believe no one wanted these little guys," Anna said sadly. "Look how excited they are to be adopted!"

The dogs did seem to have a spring in their step now compared to when we'd first seen them in the meet and greet area of the shelter. Blanche and Dorothy lifted their squishy faces into the air, tongues hanging out as they gave us their best doggy smiles.

We'd come thinking we'd get a puppy, but the minute we saw these two we'd both fallen in love with them. The shelter staff told us that they'd grown up together, but after their owner died, their kids brought them to the shelter.

"They've been so depressed," the lady at the shelter told us. "Everyone overlooks them for the cute little puppies. A lot of time we have to put the senior dogs out of their misery before they go crazy in the kennels, poor things."

As if they'd practiced it, the two dogs had looked up at us with sad eyes, one of them giving us a piteous whine.

And that's how Blanche and Dorothy conspired with the shelter staff to sucker us into adopting two senior dogs instead of one little puppy.

"Oh my God, how cute would it be if they were ring bearers in our wedding!"

I shook my head indulgently at my fiancée. "No."

"But Jolene, can't you just picture it? We can put little doggy dresses on them."

"No."

"But..."

"Don't make me paddle your ass when we get home," I teased her.

"Please," she sassed, "We both know that's not a punishment for either one of us."

Blanche stopped to pee on a tree a few feet away from the car. Dorothy waited patiently, then went to pee on the exact same spot.

Having dogs was going to be a new adventure, but after the past year, Anna and I were all about new adventures. It had been almost a year since Anna had moved in across the hall. She'd basically been living with me after we came out about our relationship to Jess, but when her lease was up this month were going to make our cohabitation official.

Then three months from now, we'd stand up before all of our friends and pledge our commitment to each other until death do us part. Our relationship might have started off as unconventional, but it worked perfectly for us.

We were good friends. Good roommates. And soon we'd be good spouses.

We put the dogs in the car, then I backed Anna against the passenger door and gave her a long, hard kiss.

"What was that for?" she asked.

"Just for being you."

She leaned forward and gave me a quick kiss of her own.

"Let's take the kids home and then you can give me that spanking."

***

Want to read about how Anna's friend Alice got together with her wife Jewel? Check out "My BFF's Sister[1]", part of the Friends to Lovers contemporary lesbian romance series. You can find more of Reba's lesbian romances at

Books2read.com/rl/lesbianromance[2]

If you liked this book, please consider leaving a review or rating to let me know.

Be sure to join my newsletter for more great books. You'll receive a free book when you join my newsletter. Subscribers are the first to hear about all of my new releases and sales. Visit my mailing list sign-up at bit.ly/RebaBaleSapphic[3] to download your free book today.

---

1. https://books2read.com/u/4NxD1J

2. *https://books2read.com/rl/lesbianromance*

3. https://bit.ly/RebaBaleSapphic

Special Preview

The Divorcee's First Time
A Contemporary Lesbian Romance
By Reba Bale

"It's done," I said triumphantly. "My divorce is final."

My best friend Susan paused in the process of sliding into the restaurant booth, her sharply manicured eyebrows raising almost to her hairline. "Dickhead finally signed the papers?" she asked, her tone hopeful.

I nodded as Susan settled into the seat across from me. "The judge signed off on it today. Apparently his barely legal girlfriend is knocked up, and she wants to get a ring on her finger before the big event." I explained with a touch of irony in my voice. "The child bride finally got it done for me."

Susan smiled and nodded. "Well congratulations and good riddance. Let's order some wine."

We were most of the way through our second bottle when the conversation turned back to my ex. "I wonder if Dickhead and his Child Bride will last for the long haul," Susan mused.

I shook my head and blew a chunk of hair away from my mouth.

"I doubt it," I told her. "Someday she's gonna roll over and think, there's got to be something better out there than a self-absorbed man child who doesn't know a clitoris from a doorknob."

Susan laughed, sputtering her wine. I eyed her across the table. Although she was ten years older than me, we had been best friends for the last five years. We worked together at the accounting firm. She had been my trainer when I first came there, fresh out of school with my degree. We bonded over work, but soon realized that we were kindred spirits.

Susan was rapidly approaching forty but could easily pass for my age. Her hair was black and shiny, hinting at her Puerto Rican heritage, with blunt bangs and blond highlights that she paid a fortune for. Her face was clear and unlined, with large brown eyes and cheek bones that could cut glass. She was an avid runner and worked hard to maintain a slim physique since the women in her family ran towards the chunkier side.

I was almost her complete opposite. Blonde curls to her straight dark hair, blue eyes instead of brown, curvy where she was lean, introverted to her extrovert.

But somehow, we clicked. We were closer than sisters. Honestly, I don't know how I would have gotten through the last year without her. She had been the first one I called when my marriage fell apart, and she had supported me throughout the whole process.

It had been a big shock when I came home early one day and found my husband getting a blow job in the middle of our living room. It had been even more shocking when I saw the fresh young face at the other end of that blow job.

"What the fuck are you doing?" I had screeched, startling them both out of their sex stupor. "You're getting blow jobs from children now?"

The girl had looked up from her knees with eyes glowing in righteous indignation. "I'm not a child, I'm nineteen," she had informed me proudly. "I'm glad you finally found out. I give him what you don't, and he loves me."

I looked into the familiar eyes of my husband and saw the panic and confusion there. I made it easy for him. "Get out," I told him firmly, my voice leaving no room for argument. "Take your teenage girlfriend and get the fuck out. We're getting a divorce. Expect to hear from my lawyer."

The condo was in my name. I had purchased it before we were married, and since I had never added his name to the deed, he had no rights to it. There was no question he would be the one leaving.

My husband just stared at me with his jaw hanging open like he couldn't believe it. "But Jennifer," he whined. "You don't understand. Let me explain."

"There's nothing to understand," I told him sadly. "This is a deal breaker for me, and you know that as well as I do. We are done."

The girl had taken his hand and smiled triumphantly. "Come on baby," she told him. "Zip up and let's get out of here. We can finally be together like we planned."

"Yeah baby," I had sneered. "I'll box up your stuff. It'll be in the hallway tomorrow. Pick it up by six o'clock or I'm trashing it all."

After they left my first call was to the locksmith, but my second call was to Susan.

That night was the last time I had seen my husband until we had met for the court-ordered pre-divorce mediation. He spent most of that session reiterating what he had told me in numerous voice mails, emails and sessions spent yelling on the other side of my front door. He loved me. He had made a terrible mistake. He wasn't going to sign the papers. We were meant to be together. Needless to say, mediation hadn't been very successful. Fortunately, I had been careful to keep our assets separate, as if I knew that someday I would be in this situation.

Through it all, Susan had been my rock. In the end I don't think I was even that sad about the divorce, I was really angrier with myself for staying in a relationship that wasn't fulfilling with a man I didn't love anymore.

"You need to get some quality sex." Susan drew my attention back to the present. "Bang him out of your system."

"I don't know," I answered slowly. "I think I need a hiatus."

"A hiatus from what?" Susan asked with a frown. "You haven't had sex in what, eighteen months?"

I nodded. "Yeah, but I just can't take a disappointing fumble right now. I would rather have nothing than another three-pump chump."

I shook my head and continued, "I'm going to stick with my battery-operated boyfriend, he never disappoints me."

Susan smiled. "That's because you know your way around your own vajayjay."

She motioned to the waiter to bring us a third bottle of wine.

"That's why I like to date women," she continued. "We already know our way around the equipment."

I nodded thoughtfully. "You make a good point."

Susan leaned forward. "We've never talked about this," she said earnestly. "Have you ever been with a woman?"

For more of the story, check out "The Divorcee's First Time" by Reba Bale, available for immediate download[1] today.

***

Want a free book? Join my newsletter and a special gift. I'll contact you a few times a month with story updates, new releases, and special sales. Visit bit.ly/RebaBaleSapphic[2] for more information.

---

1.   **https://books2read.com/u/bpznKX**

2. https://bit.ly/RebaBaleSapphic

Other Books by Reba Bale

Check out my other books, available on most major online retailers now. Go to my webpage[1] at bit.ly/AuthorRebaBale to learn more.

Friends to Lovers Lesbian Romance Series

The Divorcee's First Time

My BFF's Sister

My Rockstar Assistant

My College Crush

My Fake Girlfriend

My Secret Crush

My Holiday Love

My Valentine's Gift

My Spring Fling

My Forbidden Love

Coming Out in Ten Dates

Worth Waiting For

Menage Romances

Pie Promises

Tornado Warning

Summer in Paradise

Life of the Mardi

Bases Loaded

The Strangers Romance Series

Sinful Desires

Taken by Surprise

Just One Night

Hotwife Erotic Romances

---

1. https://books2read.com/ap/nB2qJv/Reba-Bale

Hotwife in the Woods
Hotwife on the Beach
Hotwife Under the Tree
A Hotwife's Retreat
Hot Wife Happy Life

Want a free book? Just join my newsletter at bit.ly/RebaBaleSapphic[2]*. You'll be the first to hear about new releases, special sales, and free offers.*

---

2. https://bit.ly/RebaBaleSapphic

About the Author

Reba Bale writes erotic romance, lesbian romance, menage romance, & the spicy stories you want to read on a cold winter's night. When Reba is not writing she is reading the same naughty stories she likes to write.

You can also follow Reba on Medium[3] for free stories, bonus epilogues and more. You can also hear all about new releases and special sales by joining Reba's newsletter mailing list.[4]

---

3.   https://medium.com/@authorrebabale

4.   https://bit.ly/rebabooks

Don't miss out!

Visit the website below and you can sign up to receive emails whenever Reba Bale publishes a new book. There's no charge and no obligation.

https://books2read.com/r/B-A-IDTM-DCOIC

BOOKS 2 READ

Connecting independent readers to independent writers.